CHRISTMAS IN JULY

story by **Arthur Yorinks**

pictures by **Richard Egielski**

SCHOLASTIC INC.

New York Toronto London Auckland Sydney
Mexico City New Delhi Hong Kong

ISBN 0-439-04663-7

12 11 10 9 8 7 6 5 4 3 2 1   8 9/9 0 1 2 3/0

Printed in the U.S.A   24

For Candy Jernigan
A.Y.

For Arthur
R.E.

Oh, it was beginning to look a lot like Christmas.
Snow fell like angels parachuting from Heaven. Bells jingled.
Chestnuts roasted. All was calm. All was bright. Right?

Wrong.

"Where's Donner? Where's Blitzen? Where's my pants!" Santa was hysterical.

Sydney, head helper, stepped forward. "Uh, sir? We have some bad news," he mumbled. "The cleaners, um, lost your pants."

"What!" Santa began to sweat. "Not my—"

"Yes, Boss. Your Christmas pants."

"Yumpin' yimminy!" cried Santa.

But wait! In a penthouse, on a chaise, lounging, a rich man, Rich Rump, was spotted wearing Santa's pants.

Santa himself went to investigate.

"Mr. Rump," Santa said, "I know we've never met, but I believe you're wearing my pants."

"Get lost!" Rump replied.

"Yes, but, I, I—" Santa stammered. "I need those pants."

"So? Who do you think I am?" Rump fumed. *"Santa Claus?"*
"But *I'm* Santa," said Santa. "And those are my pants!"
"You're a bum!" Rump yelled, and he swiftly kicked Santa out.
Boy, what a temper.

Undaunted, Santa took to the streets. "I'll get pants," he declared.

He went from store to store, but it was a lost cause. In Macy's, no one even recognized him.

Desperate for trousers, Santa stood on a corner calling out to busy pedestrians: "Hi. I'm Santa. Got any pants?"
Immediately, he was arrested for loitering.

At his trial, Santa pleaded: "I'm innocent, I'm innocent, I tell you. I'm Santa—"

"You're Santa?" the judge interrupted. "Where's your pants?"

"Well, I—"

"Six months!" the judge snapped.

"But—but, what about Christmas?" Santa cried as he was carried off to the slammer.

What about Christmas.

It came, but Santa didn't. No presents were piled under trees. Stockings, hung by the fire, hung empty. And Santa?

Santa was sayonara.

"He's just late," Jimmy MacDonald, a father, told his daughter. "You wait. He'll show up."

So they waited. Everybody waited. The whole world waited. Weeks passed. Months passed. Everyone sat and waited.

Nobody went to school. Nobody went to work. Shops closed. Businesses went bankrupt.

I'm telling you, by the time Santa got out of jail, the world was a mess.

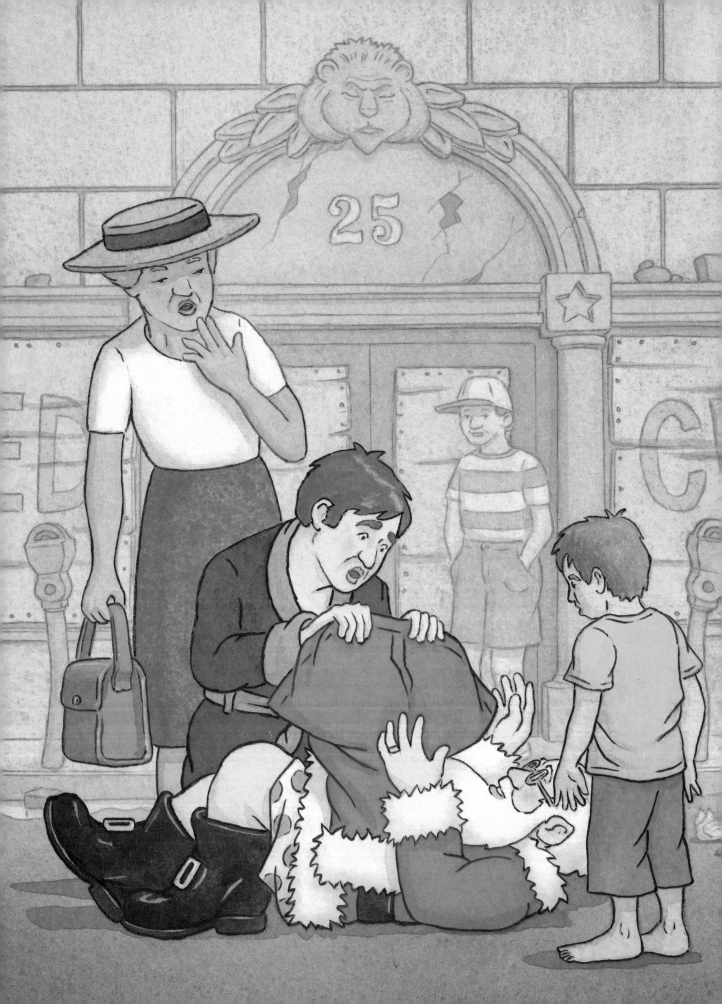

"Hey, tubby," Rump said to Santa. "You need slacks? Two-fifty." Santa was silent. "Okay, a quarter," Rump continued. But Santa was out cold.

Rump stared at the poor, pantless old man. "Gee, the pants go so well with his jacket," he thought. "And he wouldn't even need alterations." Rump's icy heart was finally melting.

"Here. Take my pants. Please," Rump offered.

Santa opened his eyes and sighed. "Such nice pants."

"They're so you," Rump said. "They're...wait a minute. You're Santa!" A crowd gathered. "It's Santa!" they hollered.

"I'm Santa!" said Santa. *"With pants!"*

Suddenly Sydney arrived, and Santa climbed into his sleigh and rode up into the sky.